MUPPETS
MOST WANTED

D0950899

Little, Brown and Company

Hachette Book Group
237 Park Avenue, New York, NY 10017
Visit our website at lb-kids.com

Little, Brown and Company is a division of Hachette Book Group, Inc. The Little, Brown name and logo are trademarks of Hachette Book Group, Inc.

The publisher is not responsible for websites (or their content) that are not owned by the publisher.

First Edition: February 2014

Library of Congress Control Number: 2013944993

ISBN 978-0-316-27764-8

10 9 8 7 6 5 4 3 2 1

RRD-C

Printed in the United States of America

THE JUNIOR NOVEL

Adapted by Annie Auerbach

Based on a script by James Bobin & Nicholas Stoller

LITTLE, BROWN AND COMPANY
New York   Boston

ONE

GESUCHT!

EVILEN FROGGEN

1000,– BELOHNUNG!

CHARAKTERISTIK

SEX: MANNLICH	RASSE: FROSCH	GEWICHT: 20KG–25KG	BLICK: SCHWARZ
ALTER: UNBEKANNT	HÖHE: 55CM–70CM	HAAR: GRÜN	TEINT: GRÜN

In the frozen wasteland of Siberia stood a Gulag—a prison for the most dangerous of criminals. Although armed guards and watchful dogs patrolled the prison, it was no match for one criminal mastermind: Constantine, the World's Most Dangerous Frog. Looking almost exactly like Kermit the Frog, Constantine had one distinguishing mark: a mole on his upper lip.

One night, Constantine karate-chopped his way out of his cell. Sirens blared and searchlights were activated. But he still escaped.

From a safe distance, he turned and looked at the prison camp. A wicked smile crossed his face as he held up a detonator. "It's time to light the lights!"

BOOM! Part of the Gulag blew up!

TWO

The Muppets had just finished filming the last scene of their movie, and Fozzie Bear couldn't have been happier. "We're together again, we got the theater, and all our fans are back!"

"To be fair, those were all paid extras," Rowlf pointed out.

"I saw a few people tapping their toes," said Fozzie.

"Those were the paid dancers," said Scooter.

Fozzie was disappointed. "Oh."

Miss Piggy saw her moment and seized it. "Since we're all here, now could be the perfect time for you and me to tie the knot, Kermie!"

Kermit ignored her. He turned to the other Muppets and announced, "Hey, everyone, we're back together, but we're all still a little rusty. So before we sign up to do anything else, I think we need to roll up our sleeves and knuckle down."

But before Kermit could finish explaining his plan, the Muppets found themselves accepting a meeting at the famed Musso and Frank's restaurant in Hollywood, California. They sat in a booth across from a man they'd just met.

"Thanks for coming. I'm a big fan. Huge," he said. "I am Dominic...International Tour Manager." He handed Fozzie his business card.

"Dominic Badguy?" Fozzie read.

"It's pronounced *Badgee*," corrected Dominic. "It's French. It means 'good man.'"

"Ooh," said the Muppets. "Cool name."

Dominic got right down to business. "Now listen, Muppets: You've conquered America."

"Not really," said Kermit. "We only did one show and—"

Dominic kept going. "You guys are HOT. You're

8

having a moment right now. What's the one thing that's inevitable about a moment? It ends."

"I don't want this moment to end!" cried Fozzie.

"So right now is the time to get out there and capitalize with a capital *C*!" explained Dominic. "It's time to go out and conquer the world! Put on an international tour!"

The Muppets cheered, but Kermit stopped them.

"Now wait a second. I'd love to do that, but we've barely gotten back together. We don't want to mess this up."

Dominic crossed his arms. "You should know I have many offers for management, so you're lucky I'm currently available."

"Does that mean you've tour-managed?" asked Kermit.

"You heard the man," Floyd said to Kermit. "What else do you want?"

"And now I want to tour-manage you guys,"

said Dominic. "I know, Kermit, you're the boss, and I would never want to interfere with that. We would split management duties. Because what you guys have is a special bond." Just then his phone rang. He excused himself to another room to take the call.

Once Dominic was out of earshot, Gonzo said, "Well, he seems like a nice guy."

Rowlf agreed. "Yeah. Humble and honest."

"I don't know," said Kermit. "I think we have to get settled first. Hone the show, develop some new material. Then maybe we go on a world tour."

The other Muppets didn't agree.

"But, Kermit!"

"I want to go on a world tour now!"

"World tours are easy! Katy Perry just did one!"

"Look, we can't just blindly jump at the first offer that comes along!" Kermit said forcefully.

Miss Piggy piped up. "Weren't you listening?

We're having a moment! This may be our only chance to become world famous!"

"That's right! Now's our chance!" agreed the others.

Just then, Dominic returned. "So, what do you say, Muppets? Ready to be world famous? No pressure. But I am a busy guy."

All the Muppets begged Kermit. "Please! Just this once!"

"Pleasen børgen schmørgen with meatballs on top!" added the Swedish Chef.

Kermit was still reluctant, until Walter came up with an idea: "We could hone our acts on the road!"

Finally, Kermit agreed. "Okay, let's do it! Dominic, you're hired. Welcome aboard."

"Yay!" shouted the Muppets.

"Thank you, Kermit. I mean, boss," said Dominic. "You won't regret it!"

Miss Piggy rushed over and hugged Kermit.

"Oh, Kermie! This is so exciting! There's nothing more romantic than a European wedding! Paris! Or Rome! Or London! Or—"

"Wedding? Piggy, what are you talking about??" asked Kermit.

But there was no time to explain. There was a Muppet world tour to plan!

THREE

B right and early the next day, all the Muppets gathered at the train station. Kermit stood in front of a beautiful, brand-new train.

"Okay, everyone," Kermit began. "If we're going on a world tour, I thought we should travel in classic style. I've booked us a tour train!"

Everyone was really excited. Kermit turned around and shook his head.

"Oh, no, not that one," he explained. "This one." He pointed behind the brand-new train, where a dingy steam train stood. The dining car had no roof, and when the whistle blew, the smokestack fell off!

"Isn't she a beauty?" said Kermit. But the others didn't agree.

Beauregard leaned out of the engine car. "All aboard!"

"Beauregard's licensed to drive a train?" asked Scooter.

"It's like a big car!" replied Beauregard. "But with no steering wheel—so it's easier!"

That didn't really comfort Scooter. Or Statler and Waldorf.

"I didn't know there was still third class," remarked Statler.

"Third class? You mean *no* class!" replied Waldorf, and they both laughed.

Just then, Miss Piggy arrived, carrying her little dog, Foo-Foo. Behind her, a porter pushed a huge cart of luggage.

"Piggy, why do you need so much luggage?" asked Kermit.

Miss Piggy shrugged. "For our honeymoon, of course."

As she passed, Kermit raised a finger to object,

but Foo-Foo growled fiercely at him. Kermit decided to keep his mouth shut for the moment.

Before long, the train departed and the Muppets were en route. First stop on their world tour: Berlin.

After several travel days, they disembarked from the train. The group followed Kermit to a tiny club. "Well, guys, this is it!" Kermit announced.

It was called the Hole in the Wall Cabaret. The marquee read DIE MUPPETS, AS SEEN ON TV!

"Die Muppets?" read Rowlf.

"Looks like they put the reviews up early," joked Statler.

"Or is that the suggestion box?" added Waldorf, laughing.

Scooter explained. "It's actually German for 'The Muppets.'"

Everyone looked doubtful as they headed inside. There, they found a theater in semi-ruins.

"The Hole in the Wall Club? More like Hole in the Ground Club!" said Miss Piggy.

Kermit tried to rally the others. "We'll start at the bottom and work our way up. I've booked us into cabaret bars and coffeehouses all across the industrial towns of northern Germany. Guys, I warned you this wouldn't be easy. But we have to start small."

"Then go huge?" Fozzie asked hopefully.

"Then go slightly less small," answered Kermit. "Then a touch less small until we're small to medium-small."

The others looked dejected and disappointed. Right then, Dominic stepped forward.

"This looks great," he said sarcastically. "I think we should all commend Kermit's effort." He clapped and got the others to clap, too. "If I may be so bold," continued Dominic, "we could consider another venue. Follow me, Muppets." Dominic led the others outside. "To be precise, *this* other venue." He gestured to the grand building before them: the National Berlin Theater.

"We don't have the money to rent the National Berlin Theater!" said Kermit.

Dominic waved him off. "We'll make it back when we sell out. Why not put it to a vote? All in favor of believing in ourselves?"

Most of the Muppets raised their hands.

"All in favor of giving up?" asked Dominic.

"That's not really what I was saying," began Kermit. But he knew it was hopeless.

Dominic beamed. "I'm glad we made this decision. You won't be sorry!"

As the Muppets all headed inside, Dominic stole a quick glance at the building next door: the German National Treasure Museum. He absently rubbed a lemur charm on his bracelet as a wicked smirk crossed his face. So far, all was going according to plan....

Backstage at the National Berlin Theater, Kermit presented the set list to the other Muppets.

"Okay, guys, since we're playing such a big theater, let's stick with what we know: We'll open with the big cabaret number. Then we'll warm up with some comedy from Fozzie, then the guest star, followed by Piggy's number, and then the finale."

Gonzo raised his hand. "Uh, Kermit, when do I do the indoor Running of the Bulls?" He pointed to some large crates, from which a lot of angry grunts could be heard.

"Sorry, Gonzo. Not this time," said Kermit.

As Gonzo turned away, clearly disappointed, Miss Piggy ran up.

"Kermie, Kermie, *one* musical number?" she asked. "I was under the impression I would have four or five musical numbers."

"Yeah, and what about our marathon jam session?" said Floyd.

Even Dr. Bunsen Honeydew jumped into the fray. "Mr. Kermit, sir, I would very much like to demonstrate my magnetic Bomb-Attractor Vest."

Kermit swiveled around. "Bunsen, why did you even invent one of those??"

"Because it's there, Kermit. Because it's there," explained Bunsen.

The Muppets began shouting over one another, asking for their acts to be included.

"Guys!" Kermit finally yelled. "We can't just do whatever we want! This is our opening night. Let's play to our strengths." He stopped and sighed. "Because, well, I didn't want to worry you guys, but if we don't sell out this theater, it would mean the end of the tour. And...maybe us."

The Muppets gasped.

Dominic walked in with box office receipts in his hand. "Good news, Muppets! We're sold out!"

Everyone cheered. Everyone except Kermit, who looked at Dominic in disbelief.

"What?" Kermit said. Then quickly covering, he added, "Um, fine. Great. Well done, Dominic." He gave a strained smile and quickly left.

Kermit was starting to feel like he was the odd one out.

FOUR

Miss Piggy barged into Kermit's dressing room, holding Foo-Foo in one arm and her wedding folder in the other. "Is this is a good time to discuss our European wedding?"

Kermit shook his head. "Not now—"

"Perfect!" said Miss Piggy, ignoring him. "I have twenty-three swatches for seat covers for the reception, eight font choices for the menu—"

"Piggy!" exclaimed Kermit. "What are you talking about?"

"I just want to involve you in some of the decision making," Miss Piggy explained.

"What about being involved in the decision to marry you in the first place?!" Kermit pointed out.

Miss Piggy put her hands on her hips. "Kermit! You never let me do what I want!"

"Well, that's because you always want too much, Piggy," said Kermit. "I haven't even proposed yet!"

Miss Piggy shrugged. "Well, you could do that on our honeymoon."

"Do you hear what you're saying, Piggy? That's crazy!" said Kermit. "You are not my fiancée. We never got engaged. How can we get married if I've never even asked you to marry me?!?"

Miss Piggy was furious. She stormed toward the door, Foo-Foo barking angrily at Kermit the whole time. Miss Piggy whirled around dramatically, her chin trembling. "You never loved me, Kermit."

"I *do* love you, Piggy," insisted Kermit. "But sometimes you drive me crazy."

Miss Piggy marched off in a huff, slamming the door. She walked right past Dominic, who was lurking in the shadows.

Back inside his dressing room, Kermit called after Miss Piggy. "Wait…I'm sorry." But she didn't hear him. Kermit moped in his dressing room for a while, and then moped on the empty stage. He wasn't only bothered by the Piggy situation. He also felt somewhat abandoned by the other Muppets.

Dominic sat down next to him. "Don't take it personally, Kermit. They still love you. They just prefer me now."

Kermit sighed. "Thanks, Dominic. That's very comforting."

Dominic tried to lighten the mood. "Hey, you know what? In these situations, I find a walk alone in the fog, maybe by a deserted canal in the former East Berlin, tends to calm the mind." He handed Kermit a map with a circle around the words DESERTED CANAL.

Kermit turned to him. "You know, a quiet stroll is not a bad idea. Let the others know I'm gone, will you?"

"Sure," said Dominic. "I promise I'll do that."

Shortly thereafter, Kermit left the theater and was soon walking along a foggy canal. He didn't notice the WANTED posters of Constantine plastered around. As the thickness of the fog increased, Kermit discovered he was all alone…until Constantine appeared right in front of him!

"Boo!" he said.

"Ahhh!" yelled Kermit.

Constantine quickly applied a fake mole onto Kermit's upper lip, then he disappeared into the fog.

"What just happened?" Kermit wondered aloud, thoroughly confused.

Just then, a German woman washing clothes noticed Kermit. She looked at him, then at the Constantine posters, and started to yell in German: *"Achtung! Sie sind hier! Evilen Froggen! Evilen Froggen!"*

That caused a group of Germans to gather, all pointing to Kermit, thinking he was Constantine. A German police van pulled up, sirens blaring. Officers ran to Kermit and grabbed him.

"Wait!" cried Kermit. "There must be some mistake. I'm Kermit the Frog!"

"Silence, Constantine!" ordered a German offi-cer. "The game is up!"

Kermit turned and saw his reflection in the window. When he noticed the mole, he screamed! Then he noticed the WANTED posters and screamed again! Before he could protest, Kermit was thrown into the back of the van. The van's destination sign quickly changed from DISNEYLAND PARIS to SIBE-RIAN GULAG.

As the van drove away, Constantine watched from the shadows. He expertly applied some green makeup to his face to cover up his own mole.

He smiled evilly. "It's not easy being mean."

Backstage at the National Berlin Theater, the Muppets ran around and rushed to be ready in time for the big show.

"Anyone seen Kermit?" Scooter called out. "It's fifteen minutes to curtain!"

Dominic walked out, with Constantine close behind. "Hey, everybody, look! Kermit's back from his afternoon stroll."

"Hello. I am Kermit," said Constantine in a weird, stilted voice. "I've been for a walk and caught a cold, which is why my voice sounds funny. I've been thinking. You guys are right. Dominic is terrific. From now on, let's go do whatever he says."

The Muppets all cheered.

"Wow!" said Fozzie. "That walk must have really helped."

Constantine turned and bowed to Miss Piggy. "Miss Pig, I have wronged you. I humbly beg your forgiveness."

Foo-Foo wagged her tail and licked Constantine's hand.

But Miss Piggy wasn't as immediately impressed. "You're not getting off that easy, buster! C'mon, Foo-Foo!"

As she sauntered away, Animal sensed something was *off* about Kermit.

"Bad frog! Bad frog!" said Animal. Then he bit Constantine's arm! Floyd had to pull Animal off of him.

Later, in Kermit's dressing room, Dominic commended his partner in crime, Constantine. "Flawlessly executed. Bravo!"

Constantine shrugged casually. "What did you expect from the World's Most Dangerous Frog? And the World's Number One Criminal, Number Two?"

Dominic sighed. "Yes, I know: *You're* Number

One; *I'm* Number Two. You've mentioned that a few times before."

"Now that we control the Muppet tour," continued Constantine, "Phase One of our plan is complete. We are now positioned to carry out the greatest burglary of all time and pin it on those gullible Muppets!" He laughed. "We're going to steal the un-stealable—the Crown Jewels of England—ensuring that my name goes down in history as the greatest thief of all time!"

"You mean *our* names," pointed out Dominic.

"Of course," replied Constantine. "My name first, then a big space, then your name."

Dominic rolled his eyes. In order to get to the Crown Jewels, hidden in the Tower of London, they'd have to steal a map, a key, and a locket, located in museums all over Europe. This would require a lot of planning. He held up a bunch of Muppet VHS tapes. "Have you studied your Kermit tapes?"

"Of course not!" said Constantine. "This is child's play for a frog of my talents." Full of pride, he walked out of the dressing room and got into position for the opening number. It was showtime!

A drumroll began....

Constantine opened the *O* of the MUPPET SHOW sign. He stuck his head out, looked at the audience...and froze in terror!

"Oh, no!" Dominic said as he watched backstage.

Constantine had the worst stage fright of all time!

Scooter whispered from the side of the stage. "Kermit, introduce the show!"

But all Constantine could manage to say was "Ahhhrrgghghh." Then he passed out!

The audience gasped, and Scooter jumped onstage to announce the show, in the same manner as Kermit normally did: "It's *The Muppet Show*! Yaaayyy!"

The show began with an elegant ballroom number. The celebrity guest host danced the waltz. In the background, Crazy Harry kept blowing up the scenery to the beat of the music!

Meanwhile, Scooter found Constantine slumped against a wall. Scooter gently touched him on the shoulder to wake him from his surprise slumber. But when Constantine woke up, he instinctively grabbed Scooter's arm and flipped him over his shoulder with his best karate move.

"Aaaahhhrrrggghhh!" cried Scooter.

"I am sorry," Constantine said quickly. "Please do not touch me. I do not like to be touched."

Scooter slowly got up. "You okay, chief?" Scooter asked. "You seem a little...high-strung."

"I am fine," Constantine assured him. "Carry on with the show. I am going for a lie-down."

With the Muppets busy doing the show, it was easy for Constantine to slip away and meet up with Dominic in the basement.

Dressed head to toe in black, Dominic looked ready for a burglary. With each loud explosion onstage from Crazy Harry, Dominic hammered through the basement wall to reach the National Treasure Museum on the other side.

Constantine picked up a hammer to join in. "It was a stomach bug; it wasn't stage fright, if that's what you were thinking, Number Two," he told Dominic.

"Of course," Dominic replied, not believing him for one second.

A few more pounds of the hammer, and they climbed through the hole into the museum!

From the museum basement, they headed up to the first floor. They walked past oil portraits, stopping in front of a painting of Colonel Thomas Blood, an angry-looking seventeenth-century Muppet. Dominic lifted the painting off the wall and cut it from its frame with a knife.

"And now to cover our tracks," said Dominic. He grabbed some priceless paintings, which set off the museum's alarm system. He hoped that would give the police the wrong idea: that the burglars were after the priceless paintings, not the Colonel Blood one.

"Let's get out of here!" Constantine yelled. He headed for the door.

Behind him, Dominic took a coin out of his pocket, left it on the floor, and fled.

The next morning, the newspaper headline told the story: *Priceless German and American portraits stolen from German National Treasure Museum!*

At the museum, police barricaded the crime scene. Sam Eagle, an interested party, flashed his CIA badge.

Interpol agent Jean Pierre Napoleon flashed a larger badge. "What is the CIA doing here? This is my jurisdiction. Not to mention my badge is bigger."

"One of the stolen paintings was on loan from the New York Metropolitan Museum of Art," Sam explained. "So this is CIA jurisdiction. Also, this is my travel badge. Here is my real badge." He removed a gigantic badge from a suitcase.

"Oh, you must have been looking at the wrong

badge," said Jean. He ripped open his shirt, revealing his entire chest covered in a badge.

Sam nodded. "You won this round, Pierre."

"My name is Jean."

"Okay, Shaun," said Sam, getting it wrong again. "Looks like we'll be working together. But that doesn't mean I have to like you."

"I didn't like you first."

"I didn't like you before I met you," insisted Sam. He looked around the crime scene. "So what have we got?"

Jean looked at his notes. "Two priceless paintings stolen, and one average painting of an obscure English colonel stolen. This has all the markings of the work of the Lemur."

"What's a lemur?" asked Sam.

"Only the second-most-wanted criminal in the world!" exclaimed Jean. "And my personal nemesis. Unfortunately for me, his identity is a mystery."

Sam shook his head. "No, literally. What is a lemur?"

"Oh, it is also a rat-monkey from Madagascar," explained Jean. Then he spotted a coin on the floor and bent down to pick it up. "Aha! Just as I suspected!" He showed it to Sam, noting the lemur that was embossed on the face of the coin. "This coin is his calling card. Ah, the Lemur…he is playing with us."

Jean pulled out a folder and handed it to Sam. "Here's the Lemur file. It's everything we have on him."

Sam opened it to find it full of Lemur coins. And nothing else.

Meanwhile, the crooks hid in a car on the Muppet train. Constantine removed the painting of Colonel

Thomas Blood from his bag and turned it over. It was blank.

"It's not there!" yelled Constantine. "You were wrong!"

"Not so fast," said Dominic. He pulled an iron from his bag. Once hot, he ironed the back of the painting. An ancient-looking map slowly appeared. "Oldest trick in the book," Dominic explained. "Write it in lemon juice. Then apply heat to reveal...Colonel Blood's map!"

Sure enough, the map was entitled "How to Steal the Crown Jewels of England. Secret Tunnels of the Tower of London, drawn by Thomas Blood, Colonel, 1670." Underneath the diagram, a set of symbols read: KEY + LOCKET = JEWELS.

Thomas Blood *nearly* stole the Crown Jewels. His second-in-command, Godfrey the Unknown, betrayed him.

"Today, the Crown Jewels lie behind the most advanced security system on the planet," Dominic said. "This map, along with Blood's key and Blood's locket, is the only way to get near them."

"Good work, Number Two," said Constantine. "What does it say about the location of Blood's key?"

Dominic scanned the page and found the name of a city: Madrid. As soon as he was able, he booked the next stop on the Muppet tour—in Madrid, Spain—and made the announcement to the group.

As the train pulled away from the Berlin station en route to Madrid, Dominic and Constantine figured out their next step.

Dominic read from the back of the painting: "It seems that Blood's key is hidden in a marble bust of his accomplice, Godfrey the Unknown, which is kept in the Statue Room of the Prado museum."

"Perfect," said Constantine. "We'll break in, steal the bust, destroy it, and grab the key."

Dominic shook his head. "It's not that simple. There are two hundred fifty busts in that room. No one knows what Godfrey the Unknown looked like."

"Of course not!" exclaimed Constantine. "He was second-in-command, so no one would care!"

Dominic, being second-in-command himself, didn't like the sound of that.

Just then, Miss Piggy interrupted. "*Excusez-moi*, Kermie. Do you have a moment?"

Constantine just stared out the window, thinking.

Miss Piggy began, "I just wanted to say that I accept your apology and now I'm ready to put that little disagreement behind us. Perhaps I was a little too eager about our wedding. So for the next few weeks, maybe we should just—"

"Pig!" shouted Constantine. "I have a question: Am I wearing a sign that says BOTHER ME?!"

In shock, Miss Piggy burst into tears and slammed the door on her way out.

"What was that?" Dominic asked.

"I was in the midst of evilly plotting," explained Constantine. "I do not like to be interrupted while evilly plotting."

Dominic sighed. "If we're going to keep up appearances, you've got to keep her happy no matter what she asks of you."

Constantine shrugged. "I am not worried. What can she do?"

The door flew open. Miss Piggy stood there, and she was fuming.

"Okay, buster," she said. "You've gone too far this time. I was trying to make nice, and you threw it right back in my face. I QUIT!"

When Constantine saw that many of the Muppets were watching, he realized that Dominic was right. He *had* to keep the pig happy. He decided it was time for Phase Two: Romance.

He walked to Miss Piggy's train car, where he found her packing.

"I don't want to see you, Kermit," Miss Piggy told Constantine.

The frog stepped forward anyway.

"I don't think you know what you want,"

Constantine said smoothly. "Because you're my lady. And I'm your man. And that's why, if you stick with me, I'll make your dreams come true."

And with that, Constantine won her over. Too bad she didn't know it wasn't the *real* Kermit the Frog.

SEVEN

Thousands of miles away, the van transporting Kermit arrived at the Gulag. Kermit was put in the main prison yard with the worst of the worst: the Prison King, Miss Poogy, and Big Papa.

"It's Constantine! He's back!" yelled the Prison King.

All the prisoners kneeled and bowed down to Kermit.

Kermit looked at all the down and dirty folks around him. "I'm not Constantine. I don't know who that is. My name is Kermit."

The prisoners all thought that was hilarious.

"Good ol' Constantine," said Miss Poogy. "Always tryin' to pull a fast one!"

"Buddy, it's been too long," said the Prison King. "Since you're back, I guess you're in charge of the prison again." He held out a handmade crown made of sporks.

"Thank you," said Kermit, taking it.

The prisoners all fell silent, in shock.

Uh-oh, thought Kermit. *What did I do wrong?*

Finally, Big Papa spoke up. "I've known Constantine for years, and he has never, ever said 'thank you.'"

"Because I'm not Constantine!" insisted Kermit.

The prisoners went wild. "He's *not* Constantine! Who would do such a thing? Let's get him! Put him in the recycling compactor!"

Kermit screamed as the prisoners rushed toward him.

Suddenly, a voice said, "Put the frog down."

Kermit was dropped on the ground. He turned to discover that the voice belonged to a beautiful but hardened Russian guard. She held a stun gun and used it on the other prisoners.

"Sorry, my finger slipped," Comrade Nadya said.

Then she shook her head. "It did not slip. That was intentional." She helped Kermit up and walked him to his cell.

"So, frog, if you're not Constantine, why do you have that mole?" she asked.

"It's not real. It's been glued to my lip," explained Kermit.

"Sure, frog," Nadya said dismissively. "Everyone is innocent in a Gulag. As far as the authorities are concerned, you're Constantine. Glue or no glue."

"Who is this Constantine guy, anyway?" asked Kermit.

Nadya took a deep breath and explained, "Abandoned as a tadpole by his mother, Constantine was adopted by the owner of Russia's largest bomb factory. (Which he subsequently blew up!) He is the world's foremost explosives expert and number one criminal. He blows up the scenes of his crimes to cover his tiny frog-sized tracks."

"Well, I can assure you: I am terrified of bombs!

Especially onstage!" said Kermit. He instantly realized his joke bombed.

"Make yourself comfortable," Nadya told him
once Kermit was behind bars. "You're going to be
here awhile. Now, lights out!"

EIGHT

Back in Spain, mayhem was brewing among the Muppets (and not the Electric kind!).

All the Muppets kept asking Scooter what the set list was going to be for that night's show. But he didn't know. So finally, he asked Constantine.

"I don't care," replied Constantine to Scooter and the rest of the Muppets. "Do whatever you want."

"What? REALLY?" exclaimed the group.

"Of course," added Dominic. "You guys are so talented you can do whatever you want."

Gonzo's eyes grew large. "Can I do indoor Running of the Bulls?"

"Yes, Zongo, you can," said Constantine, getting his name wrong.

"Really?" replied Gonzo. "Thanks, Kermit. You'll probably regret this!"

Miss Piggy put her hands on her hips. "Kermie, if he can do his thing, why can't I sing my five songs?"

Constantine shrugged. "You can. Why not?!"

"Oh, Kermie!" Miss Piggy gushed happily.

Scooter interrupted. "We haven't got time for all this stuff. We're up to a three-hour show, right, Kermit?"

"So what?" said Dominic. "Some movies are over five hours long. And everyone loves them. Well, almost everyone."

The Muppets were happy with the new longer-show idea and ran off to get ready.

Later, Scooter poked his head into Constantine's dressing room. "Kermit, it's five minutes 'til showtime. Why aren't you dressed?"

"I refuse to perform," declared Constantine. "Start the show without me."

Luckily, Dominic was nearby and stepped in to help. He pulled Constantine into the bathroom and shut the door. Scooter could hear the whole conversation.

"You must go, Number One," said Dominic. "It's vitally important."

"No!" insisted Constantine. "You cannot make me go. You're the one who must go, Number Two!"

"I can't go. I don't need to go," said Dominic. "You're the one who needs to go, Number One."

"I can't go, Number Two, if you're standing there!" Constantine said.

"Please! I'm begging you," said Dominic. "Go, Number One!"

Constantine put his head in his hands. "I can't! Not after what happened last time." He thought of the horrible stage fright he experienced.

Dominic looked him squarely in the face. "For both of our sakes, you have to go, Number One! Go, Number One!"

Outside the bathroom door, Scooter shook his

head and walked away, thoroughly confused (and perhaps a little grossed out).

A few minutes later, Constantine sat himself down in front of a TV and watched a VHS tape of an old *Muppets* episode.

"Hi, ho. Kermit the Frog here," said Kermit on the screen.

Constantine tried to mimic him. "Ho, hi. Kermit a Frog there."

When Kermit sang "the lovers, the dreamers, and me," his face was sweet and full of emotion.

When Constantine sang it, he had no expression whatsoever and got the words wrong: "the lovers, the dreamers, and cheese."

Constantine hit the STOP button. "Perfect. Nailed it." He left the dressing room and headed toward the stage.

In the wings, Scooter looked on as the Muppets took their positions for the opening number. It was chaos.

"I can't watch!" said Scooter, covering his eyes.

Nearby, Constantine peeked out at the audience. Suddenly, he started to feel woozy. He tried to snap out of it, telling himself, "You are the World's Most Dangerous Frog. Now act like it!"

It worked. He snapped into focus, walked out onstage, opened the *O* in the MUPPET SHOW sign, and announced the show. "It's *The Muppet Show* with our very special guest star, Salma Hayek! Yaaaaay!"

The audience cheered, which made Constantine feel good. After the opening musical number, he came back out onstage.

"Welcome to *The Muppet Show*. We're live in Madrid! Please welcome our first act: the Great Gonzo and the indoor Running of the Bulls!"

As the audience clapped, Constantine stood there, enjoying the applause.

"Okay, Kermit. You can come off now," Scooter whispered.

Constantine reluctantly left the stage. "When am I on again?" he asked Scooter.

"You're kind of in the whole show," replied Scooter.

"Of course. Good," said Constantine. He glanced over at the clock. "Oh, I have to go. Cover for me."

Before Scooter could argue, the frog was gone.

NINE

Down in the basement of the theater, Dominic waited impatiently for Constantine. It was the same plan as before: Go from the theater basement into the museum basement next door.

"Where have you been?" asked Dominic when the frog showed up.

"Onstage," replied Constantine just as they started to hear the bulls running above them.

As the noise level rose, Constantine used dynamite to blow a hole in the wall. Soon, they were inside the famed Prado museum, searching among two hundred fifty busts.

"Thomas Blood's key is hidden in one of these busts," said Dominic.

Constantine grinned and sang, "It's time to get things started...."

The smashing began, but after 249, there was no key. Dominic picked up the last one.

"This one says 'A Man Forgotten by History,'" said Dominic. "And he looks annoyed."

Constantine glanced over. "He looks a bit like you, Number Two."

Dominic lifted up the bust and, with a whole lot of anger, smashed it. Among the debris, he found a large iron key. On it was written COLONEL BLOOD'S KEY.

"Nice of him to label it," Constantine pointed out.

"There's more," said Dominic, reading it. "'With Colonel Blood's key, the jewels may set you free. But it is Colonel Blood's locket that you will need in your pocket. To capture the jewels.'"

"That doesn't even rhyme," said Constantine.

"He was a thief, not a poet," Dominic barked. "Give him a break."

"So where is the locket?" asked Constantine.

Dominic read the back of Blood's portrait. "The

vaults of Eire...of course! Blood was Irish. And the National Bank of Ireland keeps open-ended accounts. The locket must be in the vault of the Bank of Ireland!"

Constantine's lips twitched into a smile. "Next stop: Dublin."

As the pair scurried off, Dominic left another Lemur coin on the floor.

When they made it back to the theater next door, the audience was giving a standing ovation. Constantine ran onstage.

"I am Kermit. I hope you enjoyed my show. Good night, Madrid!" He moonwalked offstage, and the audience went wild.

All the Muppets were surprised and buoyed by the applause. They were not used to such a great crowd.

"Great show! Nice one, Kermit!" Fozzie congratulated his friend once they were offstage.

Walter scratched his head. "Guys, I'm not sure

that was such a great show," Walter said, thinking about the runaway bulls and Miss Piggy's five musical numbers.

"Well, it seems the Spanish reviews disagree with you," said Dominic. He held a few Spanish newspapers up to Walter's face. "We got five out of five *jamon serranos*!"

Walter couldn't believe it. "Wow, those reviews really came out fast." In his head, he thought it was *too* fast. Something was fishy.

Miss Piggy picked up the paper. "Oh, Kermie. Look at these reviews. I've never been happier. Thank you, Kermie. Thank you!" She covered Constantine's face in kisses.

"I do it all for you, my dear," lied Constantine. "Because you and me, we are meant to be together forever."

Before anyone could say another word, Dominic announced, "Pack up, everyone. I've just booked our next gig in Dublin."

Walter thought that was great news, since it would take some time to travel to Dublin. "Now we've all got time to rehearse." He certainly didn't want another show like the one they just had.

"Rehearse?" said Dominic. "Let's celebrate!"

Constantine looked at the assembled Muppets. "Go do whatever you want. You deserve it, comrades!"

When Sam and Jean heard about the Prado museum burglary, the two detectives sprang into action. Jean led the way to his car.

"What is this? A toy?" said Sam when he saw Jean's tiny car. "My truck could eat this car for breakfast."

However, Jean was very proud of his car, Le Maximum. "It's illegal now in most of the EU for its massive size," he explained.

As they both got into the tiny car, Sam grumbled, "I hate Europe!"

After a crazy and long ride, they arrived at the museum. It didn't take long for Jean to discover the Lemur coin. "I knew it!" he exclaimed.

"This doesn't make sense," said Sam. "Why break in, smash some worthless busts, and not steal anything? Something bigger must be going on, but what?" All of a sudden, he noticed the *Muppet Show* poster. "Wait! Those weirdos the Muppets were performing next to the crime scene in Berlin. And here they are performing right next to the crime scene in Madrid."

"You're right!" said Jean. "We must find these Muppets—before they flee the country!"

They raced back to the car and sped to the train station. They parked and flashed their badges at the Muppets. Then they took them to the local police station for interrogation.

They questioned all the Muppets one by one, but they got nowhere. Everyone's alibi was that they were part of the show, not breaking into the Prado museum. Sam had his head between his wings. Jean was so frustrated he was literally banging his head against a desk.

Finally, Sam conceded. "Maybe your Lemur hunch is correct."

Although Jean wished it were that simple, he had just discovered a flyer stating that the Muppets would perform the next night at the Dublin Theater. "Which just happens to be next door to the Irish National Bank!" he said. Then he admitted to Sam, "Maybe your Muppet hunch is correct. Come on! We must follow the Muppets to Dublin!"

TEN

One night, in his small prison cell, Kermit pulled a spoon out from under his pillow. He lifted up a large poster of Miss Piggy, ready to continue digging. But Nadya was looking out at him from the hole in the wall!

"Stop digging escape tunnel, frog!" Nadya said.

"How did you know?" asked Kermit.

"It's the first escape everyone tries," she explained, and promptly took the spoon away.

Next, Kermit tried to escape through a laundry basket. But Nadya discovered him.

"That's the second escape people try," she told him.

Kermit tried to escape through the sewer pipes, which didn't work, either.

"Give up, frog," said Nadya. "I have seen every

prison movie ever made. Even the ones in space. So you throw in towel, eh, frog?"

Kermit sighed. "I can't throw in the towel. I'm worried about my friends. We're in the middle of a tour."

"Well, maybe your friends have forgotten about you," said Nadya.

"No," insisted Kermit. "They wouldn't. They couldn't."

"Look," began Nadya. "You work in the business of shows, correct? We have the annual lighthearted Gulag Revue coming up. It is that, or they riot. Since you're here forever, I thought you might help me. I am the director."

"Well, the thing is, Nadya, I'm kind of done doing that," replied Kermit. "But thanks for the offer."

Nadya shook her head. "This is not an offer. This is prison. You are going to help me. Rehearsals tomorrow, 4 AM. Or I put you on... the Wall!"

"The Wall? Pff!" said Kermit. "Why should I be scared of a wall?"

Before he knew it, Kermit was taken outside in the freezing cold. Nadya licked him with her tongue and threw him against a giant metal wall. Kermit stuck to it. Despite struggling, he couldn't get free. He looked down at Nadya and said, "What time did you say rehearsal was?"

Nadya smiled and reached up, slowly peeling Kermit off the metal wall.

The following morning, Kermit watched the current acts from the prisoners. They were *awful*. Bad music, terrible dancing, and depressing songs.

Nadya thought so, too. She turned to Kermit and said, "Fix this, or it's the Wall!"

Kermit gulped. He nervously stood before the other prisoners. "Well...um...first of all, I'm not sure if this is the best opening number. It's always good to start with an up-tempo song and dance before going into a comedy routine. You really want to save your ballad 'til the end."

"But we like Boyz II Men," said Big Papa.

"It's the only song we all know," said the Prison King.

"I'm not learning no other song," declared another prisoner. "I'm a triple threat: a singer, a dancer, and a murderer."

As the prisoners raised their voices in protest, Kermit was reminded of the arguments he used to have with his fellow Muppet performers.

Finally, he shouted, "QUIET!!! We're holding auditions tomorrow. If any of you have a problem with that..." He took a breath. "...my door is always open."

Nadya was smitten with the stronger side of Kermit. "Thank you," she told him. "This is what we've all been waiting to hear."

"You have?!" asked Kermit.

The prisoners nodded. "Teach us, Kermit. We'll do whatever you say."

Over the next few days, Kermit auditioned and cast for the Gulag Revue. With Kermit training them, the prisoners improved during rehearsals. Even Nadya had eased up on Kermit. In fact, she'd developed a full-blown crush. He didn't know it, but she had a locker full of Kermit pictures and memorabilia.

"Ah...my green prince," she cooed at the picture. "I will never let you go...."

ELEVEN

The Muppets were all on the train headed to Dublin, Ireland, for the next stop on their world tour. They seemed to be taking Dominic's advice to celebrate, perhaps a little too much. The Electric Mayhem Band went crazy and destroyed their instruments. Bunsen and Beaker experimented on a robot. Pepe the King Prawn hosted a party in his train car. Things escalated quickly. Gonzo rode his motorcycle inside while a shark attacked the Swedish Chef. It was absolutely out of control!

The only one who *wasn't* getting crazy was Walter. He noticed that Kermit was acting a little strange. But when he asked the others about it, no one seemed to care. They were too busy having fun, too busy doing whatever they wanted. But Walter just *knew* something wasn't right. And when the train pulled into the Dublin station, he spotted Dominic out the window, looking shifty.

"Well, well, what's he up to?" Walter wondered aloud. He grabbed a trench coat and followed Dominic down the street, careful to keep himself hidden.

Walter followed Dominic as he went down an escalator, ice-skated across a pond, and even had his portrait painted by a street artist. Finally, Dominic entered a garden gnome warehouse.

Creeping into the warehouse, Walter saw Dominic sitting with two men. Walter hid behind a corner, but close enough so he could hear what was being said.

"I need this review printed on Friday," Dominic said to an Irish journalist. "It has to be super positive. Five stars."

"I won't be paid off for a review!" said the journalist, sounding offended. Then he began to laugh. "I'm joking, of course. Cash or credit?"

Dominic handed the man a suitcase full of cash. Then he turned to the other man, a theater manager.

"I need you to hand out these tickets to anyone who'll take them. You may have to pay people to come." He slid another suitcase of cash to the theater manager.

Walter covered his mouth so they wouldn't hear his gasp!

The theater manager sighed. "Last time they were here, they sold eight tickets. I'm a theater manager, not a miracle worker."

"Oh, and I want a standing ovation at the end," added Dominic. He slid a third suitcase of cash over to the men.

"Where does he keep all those suitcases?" Walter wondered aloud.

Silently slipping away, Walter made it back unseen to the train station. He barged into Fozzie's train car.

"Fozzie! Dominic is the reason we've been selling out our shows!" exclaimed Walter. "He's giving away tickets and bribing journalists to write great reviews."

"Why didn't we think of that?" said Fozzie.

Once he saw Walter's horrified look, he added, "I mean, oh, no! That's terrible."

"The question is why?" wondered Walter aloud. "And could it have anything to do with why Kermit has been acting so weird lately?"

"You think he's been acting weird?" asked Fozzie.

"I've only known Kermit a few months, but hasn't he been doing a lot more karate than normal?"

Fozzie shook his head dismissively. "It's probably Dominic's influence. Hey, want to see something funny?" He showed Walter a newspaper. On the front page, it read: *Europe's Most Wanted Frog: Constantine, Back Behind Bars in Gulag.*

Walter tried to keep his annoyance in check. "What does he have to do with what I just told you?"

"Nothing," replied Fozzie. "But check this out." He put his finger over the mole on Constantine's picture.

"Oh, look, it's Kermit," said Walter.

Fozzie nodded. Earlier, he had dropped some

guacamole on the picture and discovered the resemblance between Kermit and Constantine when the mole was covered.

Suddenly, Walter had a thought. "What if Kermit has been replaced by this Constantine guy?!"

Fozzie considered it. Then he frowned. "That's impossible. We'd all notice."

Just to make sure, he and Walter knocked on Kermit's door. When there was no answer, Fozzie said, "Everything's fine. Let's get out of here." He was scared and certainly didn't want to find out that their suspicions might be right.

But Walter held on to Fozzie. "We should look around," he suggested.

They entered the room. Fozzie went left; Walter went right. Fozzie opened a suitcase—it was full of guns! Walter opened a dresser drawer—it was full of knives and explosives!

Fozzie noticed some plans on the table labeled "Madrid Prado Museum Heist."

"Looks like he's planning some sort of comedy heist bit," Fozzie said.

"I hope not," said Walter. "Those never work." Then he headed over to a table and discovered a tub of green makeup. "Oh, no..."

Walter stuck his finger in the makeup and put it over the mole in the newspaper photo. He and Fozzie looked at each other.

"Ahhhrrrggghhhhh!!" they screamed.

"Let's get out of here!" said Fozzie.

"Not so fast...." replied a voice.

Fozzie and Walter turned to see Constantine standing at the door, glaring menacingly. His mole was showing, making it clear who he was.

Walter squared his shoulders and bravely said, "Why are you here?"

"What do you want?" added Fozzie.

Constantine's eyes narrowed. He bared his teeth at Fozzie. "You have *wock'd* your last wocka, bear!"

Was this the end for Fozzie and Walter?

TRAVELING TO GERMANY IN STYLE, THEY DISCUSS THEIR PLANS

...WHICH INCLUDE HOW TO KEEP GONZO FROM HURTING HIMSELF TOO BADLY.

LITTLE DO THEY KNOW, THEY ARE ABOUT
TO BECOME INVOLVED WITH CONSTANTINE,
THE WORLD'S NUMBER ONE CRIMINAL...

GESUCHT!
EVILEN FROGGEN

1000,– BELOHNUNG!

SACHED(I)88829832
TEILENDER
BERLINER POLIZEI
INFORMATIONSABTEILUNG

CHARAKTERISTIK

| SEX: MANNLICH | RASSE: FROSCH | GEWICHT: 20KG–25KG | BLICK: SCHWARZ |
| ALTER: UNBEKANNT | HOHE: 55CM–70CM | HAAR: GRÜN | TEINT: GRÜN |

Berlin

AND KERMIT LOOK-ALIKE!

EXHAUSTED AFTER REHEARSALS IN BERLIN,
KERMIT TAKES A STROLL TO CLEAR HIS HEAD.

CONSTANTINE SNEAKS UP ON KERMIT,
GLUES A FAKE MOLE TO HIS FACE, AND THEN DISAPPEARS.

PRETENDING TO BE KERMIT,
CONSTANTINE JOINS THE MUPPETS . . .

WHILE KERMIT IS SENT TO A FAR-OFF PRISON!

CONSTANTINE DOES HIS BEST TO WOO MISS PIGGY,
BUT SHE CAN'T HELP NOTICING THAT THERE'S
SOMETHING DIFFERENT ABOUT HER KERMIE.

EVEN FOZZIE REALIZES SOMETHING IS
WRONG WITH HIS BEST FRIEND.

BEFORE LONG, FOZZIE, ANIMAL, AND WALTER REALIZE
THAT "KERMIT" IS ACTUALLY CONSTANTINE!

WILL THE SPOTLIGHT FADE ON
THE MUPPETS FOR GOOD?

Rowlf

Janice

Kermit the frog

Statler
Waldorf

PEPE

ANIMAL

Miss Piggy
xx

Rizzo
the Rat

RIGHT ON!

The Great Gonzo!

Fozzie Bear

TWELVE

Inside the room, Constantine stepped threateningly toward Fozzie and Walter, who trembled with fear.

Suddenly, Animal came out of nowhere and tackled Constantine. "Bad frog! Bad frog!" said Animal.

On a nearby track, a freight train trundled past going in the opposite direction. Walter spotted it.

"Quick! The freight train!" he called. He and Fozzie jumped out the window, with Animal following behind. They all landed safely. As the two trains became farther away from each other, Walter looked back and saw Constantine looking menacingly at them.

"We've got to go back and warn the others!" declared Fozzie.

"I tried! They didn't believe me," replied Walter. "It's our word against his, and, well, he's fooled them all!"

Fozzie thought for a moment. "Should we go to the police?"

Walter shook his head. "We don't have any evidence."

"I wish Kermit was here!" moaned Fozzie. "He would know what to do!"

Walter looked up, then stood, suddenly determined. "You're right. There's only one frog in the world who can save us. Only one frog who can restore order, bring justice, and set things right."

"You're talking about Kermit, right?" Fozzie asked, unsure.

Walter sighed. "Yes. Kermit!"

While Fozzie, Walter, and Animal set off to find Kermit, Constantine sat in his train compartment. He was fuming. And knitting.

Dominic stopped by and immediately knew something was up. "What's wrong? You only ever knit when you are stressed."

Constantine stopped knitting an incredibly long scarf. "The bear, the little guy, and their dog are onto us."

Dominic tensed up. "How are we going to spin this?"

It didn't take them long to come up with a plan....

At the Dublin Theater later that day, Constantine and Dominic stood before the Muppets.

"Walter and Fozzie have quit the Muppets," announced Constantine.

The Muppets couldn't believe it. "What? Why?" they asked. "Wait, you can quit the Muppets?"

Rowlf thought that didn't make any sense. "Walter quit the Muppets?! We just did a whole movie where he *joined* the Muppets!"

"I, like, totally cried when he joined the Muppets," shared Janice.

"Yeah, we, like, spent A LOT of time on it," agreed Floyd.

"Look, I know this is tough," began Dominic, "but from my professional perspective, they couldn't keep up with you guys. The show will be better without them."

"It couldn't get any worse!" joked Statler.

Constantine tried to wrap up the discussion. "Well, as us showbiz hacks say, the show must... continue... in a timely fashion."

"Wait!" shouted Gonzo. "Fozzie and Walter are part of our family! We can't let 'em leave without a fight! Right, Kermit?"

Constantine made a very dramatic sigh. "I know

this is hard, Gonzo. They were my best friends. But Dominic's right: They left us."

"But, Kermie, are you sure you're okay?" asked Miss Piggy.

"I'm fine, Piggy," replied Constantine. "The important thing is you and I are together. I could never lose you. You complete me."

Miss Piggy blushed. "Oh, Kermie."

"C'mon, guys," said Dominic. "Go! Celebrate! Have fun!"

The Muppets went back to having fun. But after a while, the novelty of just having fun all the time wore off. Not having to rehearse for the show was a great idea at first, but now a lot of the Muppets were having second thoughts.

"Maybe it's just me," said Gonzo, "but is doing whatever we want to do not as much fun as we thought it would be?"

The other Muppets nodded sadly.

"Does anyone else feel like maybe Walter was right, and maybe Kermit's acting different on this tour?" Scooter asked.

"Yeah," agreed Janice. "Something is weird and, like, not in a good weird way. Like, in a bad weird way."

Miss Piggy didn't agree. "That's ridiculous! Kermit could not be more himself! He has never been more caring or devoted to me than he has been over the past few weeks!"

"That's what we're saying," said Pepe. "He hasn't been acting himself."

Miss Piggy fell silent. Could that puny prawn be right?

THIRTEEN

S am and Jean pulled up in front of the Dublin Theater for the Muppets' show. The two detectives noticed the marquee read SOLD OUT! As they took their seats, Constantine walked onstage.

"Welcome, folks, to *Kermit and His Friends, The Muppets*," announced Constantine. "Tonight's guest will come out shortly, but first a few moments with me."

The "few" moments turned into many, *many* moments. When Constantine finally left the stage and met up with Dominic inside the Irish National Bank vault, Dominic asked where he had been.

"I had to sing 'Danny Boy,'" explained Constantine. "The audience demanded it!"

Dominic wasn't really buying the story, but he didn't say anything. He finished applying explosives around an unusually large, antique safe-deposit box labeled T. BLOOD.

"Do you have the evidence to frame the bear?" Constantine asked.

Dominic held up a rubber chicken, one of Fozzie's props.

"Excellent! Our plan is coming together," said Constantine. "Where are the guards?"

Dominic explained that the bank guards (actual leprechauns!) were not at their posts because they were watching the Muppets perform next door instead!

Dominic turned to Constantine. "One thing I don't understand: Even once we have the key and the locket, how do we actually break in to the Tower of London?"

Constantine grinned. "Leave that to me, Number Two."

"Is there a secret Phase Three?" asked Dominic.

"I'm not telling," replied Constantine. He took out the detonator for the explosives, then looked at the box again. "Hmm...seems like a big box for just one little locket."

He pushed the button and *BOOM!* The box blew open. Once the smoke cleared, Thomas Blood's skeleton fell out! Constantine and Dominic screamed. Then they noticed that the locket was around the skeleton's neck and that the skeleton was clutching the locket with both bony hands. They each tried to pry out the locket.

"Ew! Ew! Ew!" cried Constantine.

"It won't budge," said Dominic, despite using all his strength.

They continued to pull and push until they heard a noise.

"What was that?" whispered Dominic.

"Abort! Abort!" Constantine whispered back urgently. Then he yanked hard on the locket, finally detaching it from the skeleton, and the pair ran out.

Sam, who had left the Muppets' show to check on the bank vault, stepped into the light. When he saw a shadowy figure in the distance, his knew his suspicions were right. He pulled out his walkie-talkie and radioed Jean. "I think I saw something!"

Meanwhile, Constantine and Dominic safely returned backstage at the theater.

"That was close!" said Dominic, out of breath.

"Too close," replied Constantine. "I'm moving up secret Phase Three." He pulled out an engagement ring with a black stone and headed toward the stage—even though the show was still going on.

"Kermit, you can't go out there!" whispered Scooter, standing by the curtain. "It's Piggy's closing number!"

Constantine didn't let that stop him. He marched onto the stage and faced the audience. "Excuse me, ladies and gentlemen. I have an announcement."

The music stopped playing as Constantine dramatically dropped to one knee.

"Miss Piggy," he began. "I want to ask you a very important question."

Miss Piggy took a sharp breath in.

Constantine continued. "Do you wish to become Mrs. Piggy? Or rather Mrs. the Frog?" He held up the ring.

The people in the audience nudged one another and tried to get a look at the ring. Miss Piggy started to tremble. "Oh, Kermie! I thought you'd never ask! I *really* thought you'd never ask!"

"So what do you say?"

"Yes! YES! YES!" answered Miss Piggy. "Oh, Kermie, Kermie. After all this time, it was finally so easy!"

The audience broke into wild applause and cheers, and Constantine slipped the ring on Miss Piggy's finger.

Constantine turned to the audience and said, "That's right, folks. It's the Muppet wedding the world has been waiting for! We're putting our world tour on hold to be married in two days' time, at the world's most romantic location: the Tower of London!"

Offstage, the other Muppets were pretty shocked.

"Kermit's really doing it," said Gonzo.

"It's, like, totally, like, a new era or something," said Janice. "And, like, an unknown one, where robots rule the world. I'm feeling very anxious right now."

They all watched as Miss Piggy hugged Constantine.

"This ring..." she began. "It's so black. It's a little ominous, to be honest."

"It's a very rare black diamond," explained Constantine. "That ring is priceless—like you, my dear."

"Oh, Kermie."

"Now you have everything you've ever wanted—and so do I," said Constantine.

Miss Piggy paused. What did Kermit mean?

"But, Kermit, you've never wanted—"

The incoming paparazzi interrupted. "Over here, Piggy! Over here!" they shouted, snapping pictures with their cameras.

Constantine grabbed Miss Piggy, and found himself enjoying the spotlight.

Under her breath, Miss Piggy said, "What's gotten into you, Kermie?"

"Love, my dear," he whispered back. "Love!"

Miss Piggy narrowed her eyes at him. *Something was not right*, she thought.

Moments later, when Constantine exited the stage, Dominic pulled him aside.

"So secret Phase Three is proposing to the pig??"

"Keep up, Number Two," Constantine said casually. "You can't put on a stupid variety show in the Tower of London. But you can get married!" He unrolled Thomas Blood's map of the Tower of London. "You see, Blood's passageways are located directly below St. John's Chapel. I realized months ago our only chance of pulling this off was a Muppet wedding!"

It didn't take long before the news was announced around the world:

Miss Piggy and Kermit to Be Wed!
Wedding of the Century Announced!
Muppets Suspend Tour!
Slow News Week! Muppets Dominate Headlines!

It also didn't take long before the Muppets had

some questions. They gathered together and found Constantine.

"Hey, chief," Scooter said to Constantine. "We've all been thinking, and well, we were wondering, after you and Miss Piggy get married, well, what's going to happen to the tour?"

"And to the Muppets?" added Gonzo.

Constantine faced them and made himself sound upbeat. "You guys don't need me. Now you have all the freedom you want. But, hey, it was a good run. Good luck. Buh-bye."

As Constantine walked away, the Muppets looked at one another, stunned.

"Did he just say what I thought he said?" asked Rowlf.

"What are we going to do without Kermit?" wondered Scooter.

Floyd shrugged. "Only thing we can do: Pack up, go to the wedding, and then head back home. Looks like it's the end of road."

FOURTEEN

I've never seen a more ridiculous crime scene!"

Sam Eagle walked through the Irish National Bank vault, shaking his feathered head.

Under some rubble, Jean spotted a rubber chicken. "The comedian bear! He was here!"

At that precise moment, Sam discovered a Lemur coin. "The Lemur—he, too, was here!" He looked at Jean. "Could the comedian bear and the Lemur be one and the same?"

"The comedian bear is the Lemur! That is brilliant!" said Jean. "I knew he was a genius."

"But why would he steal some old bones?" asked Sam.

"Hmm…" said Jean thoughtfully. He looked down at his notes. "The bones apparently belonged to one Colonel Thomas Blood, who was the only man to ever *nearly* steal the Crown Jewels of England."

Sam's eyes widened. "The Crown Jewels? Wait— where did the frog say he was getting married?"

"The Tower of London," replied Jean.

The realization hit them both at the same time:

"The comedian bear is planning on stealing the Crown Jewels!" said Sam.

"The comedian bear is planning on stealing the Tower of London!" said Jean. He blushed. "I mean the Crown Jewels."

They jumped in Le Maximum and headed for London.

Meanwhile, Fozzie, Walter, and Animal trudged through rugged, snowy mountains, searching for Kermit. It was so cold Animal had icicles hanging from his fur. Then they trudged through a blazing-hot desert. Then snow. Then desert again.

"Does it feel to anyone else like we are going in circles?" asked Fozzie.

Before the others could answer, Walter shouted, "There it is!" He pointed to a neon sign that read GULAG. THIS WAY.

As the trio continued, there was a flurry of activity inside the Gulag itself. Prisoners, guards, and Nadya the warden were packed inside a makeshift theater. There was a dingy curtain made from prison blankets, and four flashlights taped together for a spotlight. The light pointed at Kermit.

"Good evening, ladies and gentlemen, and welcome to the Gulag Annual Revue Show! Yaaaaayyy!" said Kermit.

The guards clapped politely from the audience as the music began. A prisoner came out onstage wearing a hat with a flower. He began to tell some jokes.

"What do you call a clairvoyant midget who escaped from the Gulag? A small medium at large! But, seriously, folks, it wasn't me! Haaaahh!"

Everyone laughed, not noticing Walter, Fozzie, and Animal peering in. The trio went around the side and found Kermit backstage.

"Okay, great job, everyone. Nice work!" Kermit told the prisoners. "Escapo, you're up after the ballet."

"Psst! Kermit! Ker-mit! Psst!" Fozzie whispered.

Kermit looked under his desk and was quite surprised. "Fozzie? Walter? Animal?"

"We're here to rescue you," explained Fozzie.

"Yeah," agreed Walter. "And we've got to go *right now.*"

Kermit checked that the coast was clear. "Let's go outside. You guys can't be seen here!"

He led them outside where they could talk, even though it was freezing cold.

Kermit was ecstatic to see his friends. "I can't believe you're here! It's so great to see you guys!"

Fozzie put his hand on Kermit's shoulder. "Listen, an evil frog named Constantine has taken over the Muppets and replaced you."

"What?!" Kermit exclaimed. "Constantine? Replaced me? That's terrible!"

"I knew you'd understand," said Walter.

"Kermit's back!" declared Fozzie. "Let's go!"

But Kermit didn't move. "Wait...how could you not notice that right away, Fozzie?"

"Well, he looked like you," explained Fozzie, "and he talked like you. Well, actually, he didn't talk that much like you, come to think of it. But he said he had a cold."

Kermit couldn't believe what he was hearing. "You mean all this time, no one, not one single Muppet, noticed that I'd been replaced by an evil, criminal mastermind?!?"

Fozzie grimaced. "It sounds worse than it was."

"No," said Walter, shaking his head. "It's as bad as it sounds."

Suddenly, a Gulag newspaper truck wheeled past them. A bundle of newspapers was tossed to the ground. Kermit and the others could see the headline: *Kind of Royal Wedding at Tower of London: Kermit to Marry Piggy Tomorrow at 3 PM.*

Kermit stared at the paper, stunned. "Piggy?"

His friends were just as shocked.

Kermit bent down and picked up a newspaper. "Piggy is getting married? To the World's Most Dangerous Frog? Tomorrow?" Immediately, Kermit made a decision. "Piggy and the gang are in danger! To London!"

There was only one problem: They were stuck inside the Gulag!

FIFTEEN

W e need to escape, guys," Kermit whispered. "Tonight!"

Fozzie, Walter, and Animal looked at one another.

"But how?" asked Fozzie.

Just then, a prisoner with a large burlap sack walked up to them. "You guys know where these prop pickaxes and shovels are supposed to go for the mining number finale?" he asked.

Kermit told him, just as Walter noticed a tool-shed. Inside, he and the others found *real* axes, tools, and shovels.

"Bingo," said Walter, and a plan began to form....

A short while later, Kermit was back inside and took to the stage.

"And now, ladies and gentlemen, marvel at the talents of The Great Escapo!"

A prisoner named Escapo shuffled onto the stage in manacles and cuffs. He tried to escape them... and succeeded! The guards applauded wildly as Escapo ran through the audience toward the exit.

Nadya stood up. "Oh, no you don't!" She shot Escapo with her stun gun. "Nice try, Escapo."

From backstage, Kermit saw what had happened, and now he was nervous. "Are you sure about this, Walter? I've tried A LOT of ways to get out of here."

"If we don't try, Kermit, we'll never know," Walter told him. "Just act natural. Good luck. I'll see you on the outside."

Kermit walked back onstage to huge applause. "Thank you, guys. Thank you! And now, tonight's big finale: We're going underground, working in the coal mine!"

The famous tune began playing through the speakers. Backstage, Fozzie, Animal, and Walter passed out *real* pickaxes to the prisoners as they went onstage.

"Wow, these prop axes are really heavy," said Big Papa.

Walter winked at him. "Almost as if they were real…"

"Oh…" said Big Papa, understanding. "I got it."

He and the other prisoners took the real axes and did a complicated dance routine onstage. Then they dug a real hole in the stage floor. The guards had no idea. They were on their feet and dancing, but they thought it was all part of the show. One by one, each prisoner dropped into the "mine" they had dug and disappeared!

"Time to get out of here," said Walter. So he, Animal, Fozzie, and Kermit joined in the musical number.

"Bye-bye!" said Animal, plopping down into the hole. He was the last one down.

Suddenly, the music stopped. The stage was empty and the curtain fell. Nadya and the guards gave the performers a standing ovation.

"Bravo!" cheered the guards. "Best Gulag Revue ever!"

The curtain rose, and the stage was *still* completely empty. At that moment, Nadya realized what had happened. She had been tricked!

"No!" she yelled. "Kerrrrr-mittttt!!!!!!!"

SIXTEEN

It was a bright morning, perfect for a wedding, as guests entered the chapel at the Tower of London. Crowds gathered as policemen with dogs patrolled the surrounding streets. Nearby, Kermit, Walter, Fozzie, and Animal looked out from the truck they'd stolen from the Gulag.

Kermit frowned. "The main entrance is too well guarded. I'm going to need to get in some other way." He scanned the area and noticed a service entrance, where caterers and florists were making deliveries. Quickly, Kermit got in line to pick up a flower bouquet.

"You the new guy?" the florist asked him.

"Yep," said Kermit. "I'm the new guy."

He took the flowers and hid behind the bouquet

as he made his way inside the Tower. Everything looked good—until Dominic stopped him.

"What are you doing out here?"

Kermit jumped in surprise.

"You're supposed to be getting ready, Number One," Dominic said, thinking that Kermit was Constantine. He pointed to the mole on Kermit's face. "And your mole is showing!"

Kermit quickly launched into a Constantine impression. "I know that, you...complete, um, idiot! Sorry...I mean...I'm not sorry. You are an idiot. Why do you think I am walking around with these flowers covering my face?!"

Dominic was confused. "Uh...of course, Constantine. I didn't mean anything by it." Nervously, he added, "Are we still meeting?"

"Of course we're still meeting!" barked Kermit. "I'll see you wherever, I, that's me, Constantine, last said. Good day." He left and walked inside the gates of the Tower of London. Making his way to the chapel, he opened a side door and let in Fozzie, Animal, and Walter.

"Wow!" exclaimed Fozzie. "You were terrifying back there!"

"Thanks, Fozzie," said Kermit. "It felt pretty good, actually."

Kermit knew there was no time to waste. They had to find Miss Piggy!

"Now, Walter, you take Animal and look in the chapel. Fozzie, you come with me," said Kermit. "Good luck, guys!"

The two groups split up, and Fozzie and Kermit headed for Miss Piggy's dressing room. But she wasn't there. So they headed to the groom's dressing room.

"Piggy?" Kermit said hopefully. But she wasn't in there, either.

"Kermit! These are your tuxedos!" Fozzie noticed. He reached for one but slipped, knocking over a full-length mirror. It fell and shattered!

"Shh! Someone's coming!" exclaimed Kermit. "Quick—hide!"

Fozzie dropped to the ground and pretended to be a bear rug. Kermit picked up the frame from the mirror and put it back on its stand—just as Constantine walked through the dressing room door.

Kermit noticed that Constantine was wearing a tux and quickly put on one himself.

"Ach, I hate weddings," grumbled Constantine as he looked in the mirror. But the mirror wasn't there! Instead, Kermit imitated each movement. When Constantine looked left, Kermit looked the same direction. When Constantine combed his hair, Kermit combed his own. When Constantine put on a hat, Kermit grabbed a hat that didn't match. But Constantine wasn't tipped off. He leaned close to the "mirror" to inspect the hat. Kermit moved closer, too. Their noses almost touched. Constantine was about to say something when Dominic walked through the door.

Dominic took a step forward, right onto Fozzie.

"OW! I mean—nothing!" cried Fozzie.

Luckily, Fozzie's comment was ignored.

"Let us take this convenient opportunity to review our plans," said Constantine. "Once you've stolen the Crown Jewels and framed the Muppets, ring the Tower bell five times, and we will rendezvous on the roof and make our escape in the honeymoon helicopter."

"But what will you do once you're married?" asked Dominic. "The pig'll know everything."

Constantine shook his head. "Phase Four: I do not plan to be married for long."

"But if you get divorced," began Dominic, "you have to split the Crown Jewels with her fifty-fifty—"

"I will not be getting divorced, you cretin!" shouted Constantine. "As soon as she's served her purpose: *kaboom!* It will be bacon for breakfast! And no one...no one can stop me! Ha ha!"

After Constantine and Dominic left, Kermit helped Fozzie up from the floor.

"Let's go rescue Piggy!" Kermit declared. He and Fozzie ran out of the dressing room—and right into Sam and Jean.

"The Lemur!" Jean said, pointing to Fozzie. "I have you—finally! This game is over between us, and I am the winner!"

Sam jumped in. "And Constantine! The World's Most Dangerous Frog! Captured together." He turned to Jean. "We are victorious, my French friend. Case solved!"

"Perfect!" said Jean, who had instantly changed into beach clothes. "Time for my annual eight-week paid vacation. *Au revoir!*"

As Jean left, Sam shouted after him. "Wait! Where am I supposed to put them until the mobile holding unit arrives?"

But Jean didn't hear him, or he was already in vacation mode. So Sam had no choice but to stuff Kermit and Fozzie into the tiny Le Maximum.

He handcuffed them to the steering wheel so they wouldn't escape.

When Sam left to go back inside the Tower, Kermit cleared his throat. Then he did it again. And again. And again!

"You all right, Kermit?" asked Fozzie.

"I swallowed a hairpin months ago in case something like this happened," explained Kermit. "One of those prison things you learn." He coughed up a hairpin, securing it with his lips, and then skillfully maneuvered it down to Fozzie's cuffed hand.

"Ew! It's wet and slimy!" cried Fozzie.

And then he dropped it!

"Fozzie! I had that in my gullet for three months!" Kermit said, exasperated. He looked for it on the floor, but it was out of reach.

"I'm sorry," replied Fozzie. "But that was gross!"

In the distance, the two friends could hear Big Ben chime. It was three o'clock.

"The wedding! It's starting!" exclaimed Kermit.

Fozzie looked at his friend. "Sorry, Kermie. We tried. We really did."

Kermit hung his head. How was he going to save Miss Piggy now?

C onstantine and Dominic walked down a hall-
way inside the Tower of London.

"You should know, Number Two," began Constantine. "I've hired us some help, to keep you
honest. Number Twos have a habit of betraying their
Number Ones. Here, meet your accomplices." He
opened a door and inside stood a Muppet named
Bobby Benson, surrounded by his band of babies.

"Salutations," said Bobby coolly. "Babies, meet
your new boss."

The babies all looked up at Dominic and said,
"Goo goo, ga ga."

Constantine smiled wryly. "Genius, I know.
Who would suspect babies of stealing the Crown
Jewels? Look at their sweet faces!"

Dominic looked closely at their smushed faces

but didn't think they were sweet at all. But he knew he had no choice. As he headed off with the babies, Constantine wished him good luck.

Dominic and the babies turned a corner and reached a dead end. Dominic looked at the map, confused. Then he brushed away some dirt on the wall, revealing an ancient-looking keyhole. He took out Thomas Blood's key, put it in the hole, and turned it slowly. Down by his legs, a small hidden doorway opened.

"Wow, people really were smaller in the old days," he said. "In you go, li'l dudes."

The babies crawled down the dusty, cobwebbed passage. It was clear they had done this kind of thing before as they moved in strict formation. One of them made a hand signal and popped out a stone block. Then they threw down a rope made of baby blankets. One by one, and in complete silence, they climbed down into the lobby where the Crown Jewels were kept.

Once the babies were all in the lobby, they crawled toward the front door. The door's lock was far above their heads. What to do? They quickly formed a baby pyramid, and the top baby opened the lock. Dominic was on the other side of the door. Once he heard the *click* of the lock, he dashed inside, closing the door behind him.

Dominic spotted the Crown Jewels at the far end of the room, sparkling and shimmering in the light. He took a step toward them, when suddenly a baby's hand shot out, stopping him.

"Goo," said the baby, but actually meaning, "Wait!"

"What is it? We don't have time!" Dominic said impatiently.

A different baby tossed a sack of dust in the air, revealing a terrifying spiderweb of security lasers.

Dominic rolled his eyes. "Oh, come on! Not a laser web!" He thought for a moment and turned to the babies. "Go get the suspend-y rope-y thing and my cool skintight outfit."

The babies did what they were told, and soon Dominic was all decked out in his special outfit. Attached to a wire from above, he elegantly danced through the web of lasers, careful not to set one off. When he was at last in front of the Crown Jewels, he fit Blood's locket into an ancient coat of arms in the wall. There was a whirring and a clicking...then silence...

Then all the glass cases holding the jewels opened! Dominic dropped down next to the Crown Jewels, grinning wolfishly.

"Thank you, Thomas Blood!" he said gleefully.

EIGHTEEN

Kermit was going crazy. He and Fozzie were *still* handcuffed inside Le Maximum. Then things got worse: They could hear the beginning music from "The Wedding March."

"We've got to do something!" exclaimed Kermit.

"Argh!" grumbled Fozzie. "This is so frustrating!" In protest, he banged his foot on the floor of the car—and his foot went right through!

"Would you look at that?" said Fozzie. "Now *that's* a poorly made car."

Kermit looked down and pushed both his feet through the floor. "Let's get out of here!"

Through the car's now-open floor, the pair used their feet and "walked" the car closer to the Tower. With some more pulling and pushing, they extracted themselves from the car but were still attached to the steering wheel.

"Wait a second," Fozzie said suddenly. "It's made of marzipan!" He took a bite of the steering wheel, quickly freeing them both.

Nearby, a basement window in the Tower opened and Walter stuck out his head. "Psst! Kermit! This way!"

Kermit and Fozzie ran toward the window—and it was just in time, for Sam spotted them fleeing.

"Code red! Code red!" Sam yelled into his radio. He was trying to reach Jean. "Come back from vacation! Constantine and the Lemur have escaped. They are on the loose!"

Inside the Tower chapel, Constantine waited at the altar. As the music played, Miss Piggy walked down the aisle toward him, looking nervous.

The vicar stepped up in front of them. "Dearly beloved, we are gathered here today to witness the union of this pig and this frog."

Miss Piggy looked at Constantine; he just looked at his watch.

"Do you, Kermit the Frog, take Miss Piggy to be your lawfully wedded wife, in sickness and in health, so help you God?" asked the vicar.

"Yes, yes, I do!" Constantine said eagerly.

The vicar continued. "And do you, Miss Piggy, take Kermit the Frog to be your lawfully wedded husband, in sickness and in health, so help you God?"

Miss Piggy hesitated.

"Just say 'I do,'" whispered Constantine. "This is what you've always wanted, *right*?"

"I do...?" said Miss Piggy.

"Was that a question?" asked the vicar. "Because if it's posed with an up inflection, then it doesn't legally count."

"It wasn't a question," Constantine proclaimed.

"Let the lady answer," said the vicar.

Miss Piggy hesitated again. Something didn't feel right to her. She looked at Constantine, who forced a Kermit-like smile at her. She smiled back, then turned to the vicar.

"Could you repeat the question?" she asked. "I think I'm ready to answer now."

Suddenly, a trapdoor in the floor opened (thanks to Fozzie!), and Constantine fell through. Kermit then took Constantine's place at the altar.

"Piggy! It's me, Kermit! We have to get out of here!" exclaimed the real Kermit. "The wedding is off!" He reached for Miss Piggy's hand, but she recoiled.

"What? Kermit, no!" she shouted. She thought Kermit was getting cold feet and didn't want to marry her.

"Piggy, please! I'll explain later," said Kermit.

"I CANNOT BELIEVE THIS, FROG!" exclaimed Miss Piggy.

Just then, a small door in the altar opened up, and a green hand reached out. It grabbed Kermit and pulled him through the opening. Then Constantine took Kermit's place.

"I'm sorry, my dear!" Constantine said to Miss Piggy. "Forgive me!"

"What is going on at MY WEDDING?" demanded Miss Piggy.

Constantine tried to calm her down. "Nothing, darling. Let's continue."

Suddenly, Walter swung through the air on a rope. He picked up Constantine and dropped him into a net in the rafters. Animal pulled on a rope— now Constantine was trapped!

"Catch froggy! Catch froggy!" Animal cheered.

Kermit reappeared through a side door and ran toward Miss Piggy. "Piggy, listen to me," he began.

"That's not me. I'm me. He's Constantine, the World's Most Dangerous Frog."

Miss Piggy spun around and saw Constantine fall directly on top of Kermit. The evil frog had chewed through the net!

Miss Piggy gasped as she stared at the two frogs.

The Muppets in the pews gasped, too.

"Two Kermits?" said Scooter. "Well, that sure explains a lot."

"I knew it," said Floyd. "No one has a cold for that long!"

"Or that bad of an accent, okay," added Pepe.

"Two Kermits?" said Statler.

"My nightmare!" finished Waldorf.

Miss Piggy looked at the two frogs, her mind reeling.

"TWO Kermits?!?! How can there be TWO KERMITS?!? And here I was worrying about rain! Of all the ways to ruin a wedding, this has got to be the most creative: two Kermits!!"

Kermit stepped forward. "No, just one Kermit—me."

"He's lying!" shouted Constantine. "I'm the real Kermit. He's an imposter." He turned to the other Muppets and said, "I let you do whatever you want! Because I love you!"

Kermit shook his head. "Love isn't about doing what everyone wants. Love is about doing what you know is best. Now I know I can't be loved all the time. Heck, I can't be *liked* all the time." He looked at Miss Piggy. "But I love you." He turned back toward the other Muppets. "*All* of you. Even when you drive me crazy." He took another step toward Miss Piggy. "And some of you *because* you drive me crazy."

Miss Piggy stared at Kermit, wondering if it was really him.

Constantine stepped between them. "Don't listen to him! I'm the real—"

"EVERY KERMIT BE QUIET!" ordered Miss

Piggy. "I'm going through a lot of emotions right now. I've waited my whole life for this moment, so why aren't I more happy? I mean, I'm not even crying *at my own wedding*! Is this all just what I *thought* I wanted?"

Miss Piggy turned to Constantine. "Are you just the Kermit I *thought* I wanted?"

She took a deep breath and said, "There's only one sure way to settle this."

Silence fell upon the chapel. The Muppets all leaned forward with anticipation.

Miss Piggy turned to Constantine and in a very businesslike tone asked, "First Kermit, will you marry me?"

"Yes! Of course!" exclaimed Constantine. "Let's go! The helicopter is waiting, my love."

Miss Piggy turned to Kermit. "And you—other Kermit—will you marry me?"

Kermit gulped. "Um...well...I...it's just..."

Miss Piggy smiled. *"That's my Kermit!"* She covered him with kisses as the other Muppets broke out in applause.

All of a sudden, the Tower bell began to ring. Constantine knew that was a signal from Dominic.

"That's right, Muppets!" Constantine said, stepping forward. "I am Constantine. The World's Most Dangerous Frog and Number One Criminal and a thousand times better frog than this Kermit person! You gullible idiots didn't even realize I was setting you up! None of those five-star reviews was real. And those standing ovations? I *paid* for them!"

The Muppets looked stunned.

"And now," continued Constantine, "I only have one more thing to say to you fools…" In his best Kermit voice he said sarcastically, "Good night, folks. Yaaaaay!!!"

He pulled out a detonator that looked like a TV remote. Pushing a button, he activated it. A *beep*,

beep, beep started sounding from somewhere in the chapel.

"What's that?" wondered Scooter.

"It's a bomb!" exclaimed Kermit. "He blows up all his crime scenes. We have to find the bomb!"

NINETEEN

The Muppets frantically searched for the bomb inside the Tower chapel.

Bunsen had an idea. "This is where my patented magnetic Bomb-Attractor Vest can aid us, and Beaker is conveniently wearing it."

"Meep?" said Beaker.

Bunsen hit a button, and the magnetic Bomb-Attractor Vest Beaker wore began to hum. Miss Piggy, pulled by the ring on her finger, flew toward the vest and became attached.

"Aaaagh! What's happening?" cried Miss Piggy.

Beep, *beep*, *beep* went the bomb.

"Meep! Meep! Meep!" went Beaker.

"Wait!" yelled Kermit. "Piggy's wedding ring is the bomb!"

"Get it off! Get it off!" Miss Piggy said frantically.

Kermit yanked on the ring, but it wouldn't budge. The Swedish Chef rushed over and started buttering Miss Piggy's finger, hoping that would help it slide off. Half of the Muppets pulled on Miss Piggy, the other half pulled on Beaker. The beeps (and meeps) continued. Time was running out!

On the count of three, the Muppets pulled hard one last time. The ring came off Miss Piggy's finger with a *pop*!

Beaker fell backward and crashed through one of the chapel's stained glass windows.

The vicar put his head in his hands. "That's only eight hundred years old."

"Meeeeeeeeeeeeeeeeeeeeeeeep!" shouted Beaker as he—and the ring—fell toward the Thames river below. Once the bomb hit the water, it exploded harmlessly. Beaker wasn't hurt at all and rode the geyser of water created by the explosion. "Meep! Meep! Meep!" he exclaimed.

From the chapel window, all the Muppets cheered.

"Well done, Beaker!" Bunsen called out. "At no point were you in any danger." Then he turned to the Muppets next to him and whispered, "He was in *a lot* of danger!"

The Muppets turned away from the window to see Kermit smiling at them.

"Boy, I missed you guys!" said Kermit.

The Muppets were thrilled to see their old friend.

"Wait a minute," said Kermit. "Where did Constantine go?" He looked around and noticed Miss Piggy was also missing.

"Kermit! Help!" came Miss Piggy's voice from above.

Kermit looked up. "She's on the roof!"

Sure enough, Constantine had tied Miss Piggy's hands together and dragged her to the roof. "Keep moving, pig," he snarled, leading her toward a waiting helicopter.

Constantine opened the door to the helicopter.

Already sitting inside was Dominic—proudly wearing a furry lemur outfit.

"Number Two! What are you wearing? You look ridiculous," said Constantine.

Dominic ignored the insult. "I am...the Lemur! And the world's *new* Number One Criminal," Dominic declared. "That's right. This is where I double-cross you. Good-bye forever, *former* Number One!"

Constantine narrowed his eyes. "First rule of double cross: You don't announce the double cross before you double-cross! It's not even a rule because it's so obvious!"

With a devilish grin, Constantine pressed a button on his remote and happily watched Dominic's seat (along with Dominic) eject sideways out of the helicopter.

"You are literally the worst Number Two I have ever had!" Constantine called after him. Then, dragging Miss Piggy, he grabbed the Crown Jewels, jumped in the helicopter, and flipped on the rotors.

Kermit and the other Muppets ran onto the roof just in time to see the helicopter start to lift off.

"He's getting away!" shouted Fozzie. "What are we going to do?"

Kermit took charge. "I'm going to stop that helicopter!" He ran toward it, with the other Muppets following behind.

As the helicopter hovered in the air, the Muppets jumped to try and grab any part of it. They all missed and landed safely on the ground—except Kermit. He managed to grab hold of the helicopter.

"Whoa!!!" cried Kermit as the helicopter ascended.

"Kermit!" Walter yelled from the ground.

"We've got to do something! We've got to help Kermit!" said the others.

"Quick!" said Fozzie. "Somebody think of a brilliant Kermit-saving idea!"

Up in the sky, Constantine looked down to see Kermit holding on. Miss Piggy noticed, too.

"Kermit!" she squealed, struggling with the binding around her hands.

Even though he was barely holding on, Kermit adopted a brave tone. "Give up, Constantine. I've got you now!" He struggled to get to the cockpit floor.

Constantine smiled wickedly. "Bad move, frog." He raised his foot and stomped down on one of Kermit's hands. Now Kermit was hanging on by only one hand.

From below, Kermit heard a voice: It belonged to Gonzo. "Hang on, Kermit! We're coming!"

Gonzo and Scooter and Sweetums and all the other Muppets were standing on one another's shoulders—they had made a Muppet ladder!

"Now!" Gonzo yelled. That was the signal for the other Muppets to hang on tight while Gonzo dived forward toward the helicopter. His hands fell short of the helicopter, but he latched on with his nose instead! "Got it!" cried Gonzo. That helicopter wasn't going anywhere now!

Kermit was now dangling by one hand from the helicopter. Constantine looked down and said, "Good-bye, Kermit the Frog." He stomped on Kermit's other hand.

Kermit couldn't hold on and fell with a loud "Arrgghh!"

"Nooooo!" cried Miss Piggy. Desperately, she looked down to try and see where Kermit landed.

In the cockpit, Constantine pulled up the steering stick. "Checkmate. Let's go, pig."

As the helicopter began to pull away, Miss Piggy sobbed. Her beloved Kermie was gone.

U h-oh," said Gonzo.

As the top of the Muppet ladder, Gonzo's arms started to grow longer. He held on tightly to the helicopter.

Just then Sam and Jean, who Sam had reached on vacation, appeared on the roof.

"Muppets! You are all under arrest!" shouted Jean. "Wait—they are getting away!"

Then the bottom of the Muppet ladder lifted off the roof.

"Not so fast!" called Sam. "We have you now!"

Sam grabbed Sweetums's feet, who was at the bottom of the ladder. But then Sam began to get dragged upward, too.

"Help!" Sam called to Jean.

Jean ran over and grabbed Sam's feet. "I have

you, *mon ami*, do not worry," he reassured Sam. Now the two detectives were part of the Muppet ladder.

The Muppet ladder went taut, looking like a kite string stretching across the night sky.

Up above, the helicopter suddenly halted with a shudder. Constantine pulled on the steering stick, but it was no use. He looked down and spotted the Muppet ladder, which was preventing him from escaping.

"Muppets?!?" he snarled. "Don't they ever give up?"

While Constantine was distracted, Miss Piggy stopped crying and began to furiously rub her ropes on a sharp edge she spotted on a column in front of her.

Meanwhile, Constantine was determined to get away. He opened the throttle even more. "Full power!"

The helicopter started to inch upward again, and a grin spread across Constantine's face. The Muppet ladder was almost at its breaking point.

"Can't...hold...on...much...longer..." said

Fozzie. Then his hand let go and the chain began to fall apart. A couple of the chickens fell out of the ladder but flew away to safety.

"He's going to get away!" cried Scooter as the helicopter lifted slightly.

And then...

A green hand appeared over the top of one of the Tower of London battlements. Then another hand. Then a frog's face. It was Kermit! He looked steely and determined.

"Papa's sprung and he's MAD!" said Kermit.

Walter looked down from the ladder and spotted him. "Guys! It's Kermit! He's alive!"

Rowlf nodded. "And way badder than before!"

The Muppets all cheered. Kermit made his way to the Muppet ladder and started to climb.

"Go get him!" Fozzie told Kermit as he climbed past.

Up in the helicopter, Constantine was still trying to pull away. He looked down and saw Kermit climbing the ladder. "The frog? But how?" he wondered aloud.

"Kermie! You're okay!" exclaimed Miss Piggy.

But Constantine wasn't about to be beaten. He grabbed an old-school pistol from his bag and fired it at Kermit.

"Look out!" yelled Miss Piggy.

Kermit dodged the bullet and continued to climb upward.

"Sorry, excuse me," he said as he stepped on the other Muppets' faces. "Coming through. Pardon. Oops. Sorry about that."

As Constantine tried to reload the gun (which took *forever* because it was so old), Kermit made it into the cockpit.

"Finally!" said Constantine, gun reloaded. He aimed the barrel right at Kermit, who gulped. "You don't know who you're dealing with. I am the World's Most Dangerous Frog!"

At that moment, Miss Piggy finally cut through

her ropes. "Oh, brother!" she said directly to Constantine. "You may be the World's Most Dangerous Frog, but you're still a FROG! Hiiiii-ya!" She leaned forward and grabbed Constantine by the legs, smashing him left and right in the cockpit, making the gun fly out of his hands.

"No! One! Tricks! Me! Into! Marrying! Them! And! Then! Hurts! My! Kermie!" she said, a smash with each word.

When she let go, Constantine swayed back and forth. "What a woman!" he said in a daze.

"Yep, MY woman!" Kermit told him. Then he pushed Constantine over with the gentlest of taps, causing the criminal to fall backward and crumple on the floor.

Kermit turned to Miss Piggy. "I'm sorry I ruined your wedding."

"Oh, Kermie," she said. "I'm so glad you did." She smiled and hugged him and they shared a kiss.

"Now...um...how do we land this thing?" Kermit asked.

"Oh, that's easy," replied Miss Piggy. She reached over and pressed the autopilot button, and the helicopter landed itself.

Once Kermit and Miss Piggy disembarked from the helicopter onto the chapel roof, they were met with cheers and whistles.

"We did it! Hooray for us! Kermit's back!" the Muppets yelled. "Time for another finale!"

"Congratulations, weirdos!" Sam said to the Muppets, holding Dominic in custody.

Jean handcuffed Constantine, and the two criminals were taken away. The two detectives were proud they caught Constantine, as well as the Lemur!

Kermit turned to Miss Piggy. "Well, I guess you could say justice prevails and love conquers all. Now let's get back to our finale—"

A voice interrupted them. A Russian voice. "There they are! Arrest them! Arrest them all!"

It was Nadya, leading a squad of guards.

Kermit was shocked. "Nadya? Wait, for what?"

"For breaking my heart," Nadya said, too quickly. "I mean…for breaking out of the Gulag. That's illegal…I think. You'll get twenty years, maybe thirty. You and all your little accomplice friends."

Kermit had to think fast. "How about this: six months, and I'll let you sing a solo at the end of the movie?"

"Deal!" Nadya agreed.

The guards waded in and began arresting Muppets.

As usual, Kermit tried to see the bright side of things. "C'mon, guys. This is not so bad. Now we have six months together to rehearse and perfect our new show!"